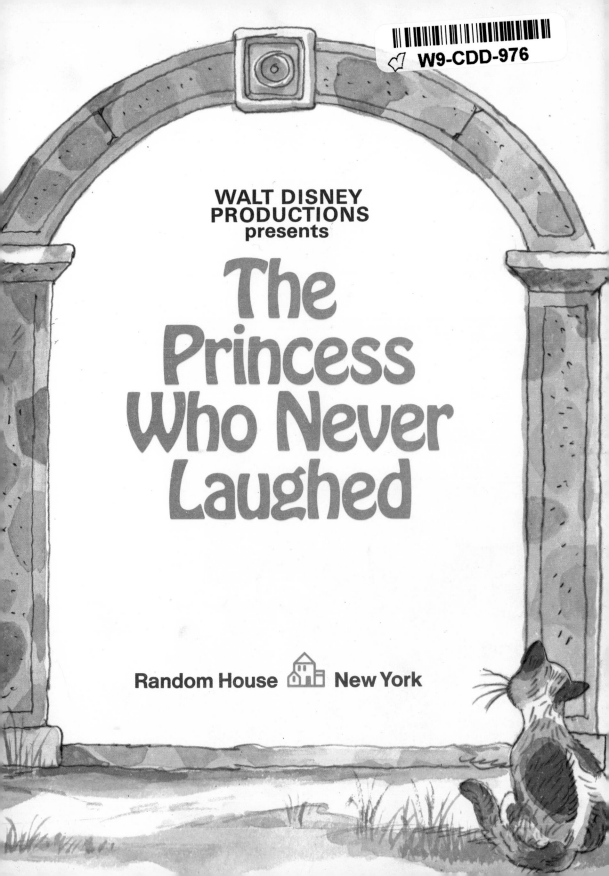

**WALT DISNEY
PRODUCTIONS**
presents

The Princess Who Never Laughed

Random House New York

Copyright © 1974 by Walt Disney Productions. All rights reserved under International
and Pan-American Copyright Conventions. Published in the United States by Random
House, Inc., New York, and simultaneously in Canada by Random House of Canada
Limited, Toronto.
Library of Congress Cataloging in Publication Data
Disney (Walt) Productions. The princess who never laughed. (Disney's wonderful
world of reading, #24) By always doing the right thing at the wrong time, Goofy
eventually succeeds in making the princess laugh. [1. Humorous stories. 2. Fairy
tales] I. Title. PZ8.D632Pr [E] 74-14699 ISBN 0-394-82565-9 ISBN 0-394-
92565-3 (lib. bdg.)
Manufactured in the United States of America   1 2 3 4 5 6 7 8 9 0

There once was a princess who never laughed.
She never even smiled.
The king brought clowns to the castle.
One made funny faces at the princess.
Another stood on his head.
One tickled her nose with a feather.
Still, the princess did not laugh.

Near the castle lived a poor woman and her son.

The son had his own way of doing things.

If his mother told him to wash carrots,
he scrubbed them on a washboard!

He was such a funny fellow that people
called him Goofy.

One day Goofy's mother looked in the cupboard.
There was barely enough food for the mice!
"Goofy," said his mother, "we have nothing
but stale bread for supper. Go to the castle and
ask for a job!"
"Cheer up, Mother," said Goofy. "I'm on my way."

When Goofy reached the castle,
he saw the princess sitting in her window.
Goofy smiled at her.
But she did not smile at him.

"I wonder why the princess
does not smile?" thought Goofy.

Goofy was so busy
looking at her
that he did not watch
where he was going.
He tripped on
a large stone.

His hands went one way.

His feet went another way.

Goofy landed on his nose with a thud.

Now the princess saw
this funny sight.
Do you think she laughed?
No. She did not even
smile.

At the royal chicken coop, Goofy found a job.
He gathered the royal eggs all day.

When Goofy's work was done, the chicken keeper
gave him some fresh eggs.

"Boy, oh boy," said Goofy.

"Fresh eggs for supper."

Away he ran to show them to his mother.

But Goofy did not watch where he was going.

He tripped again on the same stone.

His feet went one way.

His hands went another way.

The eggs flew into the air.

Goofy scrambled to catch the eggs.

As soon as he caught one,

another slipped out of his hands.

CRACK! WHACK! SPLASH!

Now the princess saw Goofy
juggling the eggs.
 And it was a funny sight.
 But do you think she laughed?
 No. She did not even smile.

"You silly," said Goofy's mother
when she heard about the broken eggs.
"If you had put the eggs in your big hat,
you could have brought them safely home."

"Cheer up, Mother," said Goofy.
"I will do that next time."

The next day Goofy worked in the royal dairy.
All day he milked the royal cows.

When Goofy's work was done, the cow keeper
gave him a pail of fresh milk.

"Wow!" said Goofy. "Fresh milk!"
Away he ran to show it to his mother.

At the castle gate, Goofy remembered
what his mother had said.
So he poured the milk into his big hat.

Then Goofy put his hat
back on.

SWOOSH! The milk splashed
over him.

Into his ears...
Down his chin...
It even trickled
under his collar!

Now the princess was in her window.
And she saw this funny mess.
But do you think she laughed.
Not the princess. She did not even smile.

"You silly goose," said Goofy's mother
when she heard about the milk. "If you had
carried the pail in your hands, you could
have brought the milk safely home."

"Cheer up, Mother," said Goofy.
"I will do that next time."

All the next day
Goofy worked, feeding the royal pigs.

When his work was done, the pig keeper
gave him a wiggly little piglet.

"A royal piglet," cried Goofy.

He could hardly wait to show his mother.

Remembering what she had said,

he tried to carry the piglet in his hands.

But the wiggly piglet was slippery.
It wiggled out of Goofy's hands.

The piglet ran through a mud puddle.
Goofy splashed through the mud, too.

The piglet ran into a haystack.
Goofy went right in after it.
But the piglet was too fast for Goofy.
It got away.

The princess looked out
her window.
There stood Goofy,
covered with mud and straw.
Do you think she laughed?
Not the princess.
She did not even smile.

That night Goofy's mother met him at the door.

Goofy told her how he had lost the piglet.

"Ninny," she said, "have you no sense at all?"

"If you had held onto the rope, you could have pulled the piglet home behind you."

"Cheer up, Mother," said Goofy.

"I will do that next time."

The next day Goofy found a job
in the royal kitchen.

All day he washed the royal dishes.

When the work
was done,
the cook gave Goofy
a fine fish.

"When Mother sees this fish," said Goofy,
"she won't be angry any more."
Then Goofy remembered what his mother had said.
Carefully he tied a rope around the fish.

Away he went, pulling the fish behind him.

When the royal cats smelled the fish,
they all came running to get a bite.

Goofy's fish was
nothing but bones
by the time he passed
the princess.
Do you think she laughed?
Not the princess.
She did not even smile.

That night Goofy told his mother
how he had lost the fish.

"Nincompoop," she cried. "You should have
carried the fish on your shoulder."

"Cheer up, Mother," said Goofy.
"I promise to do that next time."

Bright and early the next morning,
Goofy went to the castle.

This time he found a job cleaning
the royal barn.

He worked hard all day.

Goofy did such a fine job, the barn keeper
gave him a royal cow.

"This cow will make Mother rich!" said Goofy.
"But how will I ever get it home?"

Then he remembered his mother's words:

"You should have carried the fish on your
shoulder."

Goofy put his hat on the cow's head.

Next he tied his coat around the cow's neck.

Then he got down on his hands and knees
and crawled under the cow.

Goofy tried to stand up.
"This cow is heavy," he said.
Goofy huffed and puffed.

At last Goofy stood up.

Sure enough, the cow was on his shoulders.

Now the princess was looking out her window.

She saw Goofy coming up the road
with his cow.

And do you know what happened?

She laughed!

She laughed so hard
her stomach hurt.

She laughed so loud
her ears ached.

She laughed
and laughed
and laughed.

The king could not believe his ears!

"If that fellow can make the princess laugh, he should be here all the time," he cried.

So the king called for Goofy.

"Will you come to live in the castle?" he asked.

"Sure, I'd like that," said Goofy.

"If my mother can come, too."

The very next day Goofy and his mother came
to live in the castle.
And there they lived happily ever after.